Love Me Right

J.M. GOODRICH

Love Me Right

J.M. Goodrich

About the Author

J.M. Goodrich is a native of Michigan's beautiful upper peninsula. She loves spending time outdoors as much as she can with her family when she's not reading or writing. She has been published in several different anthologies and novels of her own. She has written stories of romance, fantasy, and horror. In addition to her love of writing, she has a passion for music, and an obsession with The Beatles.

One

SARAH MARTIN LIVED in a modest one-bedroom house that she had just recently rented. It was on a quiet street, and she absolutely loved it. Quiet was just what she wanted in her life right now. She lived a simple life, enjoying such things as relaxing with a good book, listening to soothing classical music, or her latest hobby - jogging.

Like she has done every other morning, Sarah finished her light breakfast, cleared away the dishes, and laced up her running shoes. She tied her long brown hair back before stepping out the door. The morning sun hit her face and she knew it was going to be a great day. She smiled to herself before getting started on her warm ups and stretches.

After she was sure her body was all stretched and

ready, Sarah clipped on her portable water bottle and took off down the road at a slow pace. Sometimes she would continue the slow jog all the way through. She hated the rushed feeling life seemed to always have nowadays. Sometimes it was nice, and necessary, to stop and smell the flowers.

Sarah continued along her usual route, calling out 'hello' as she passed her neighbors out in their yards, washing their cars or watering their plants. Everyone in her neighborhood seemed friendly and always cheerful. It made her feel. . . safe.

There wasn't a cloud in the sky, so before too long the day would grow hot. This is why Sarah preferred to jog in the morning. That, and the stillness. Besides the occasional neighbor fiddling around in their yards and the few cars that drove past, she basically had the roads to herself. No one tried to stop her and engage in conversation, or to ask her for a favor. There was no one to bother her or try to steal her time and energy.

A few months ago Sarah had picked up her life and moved from the noisy, fast-paced streets of New York to the small town of Bright Wave, on the southern coast of Maine. This was a huge change for her, but in her mind, it was exactly what she needed. Sarah rarely traveled. Although this wasn't a big move geographically, for someone who never left her hometown, this was like a move across the country.

Not knowing anyone and being able to start over again was the main draw of this small town. The extremely low crime rate and breathtaking scenery weren't too bad either.

As the day grew hotter faster than normal, Sarah detoured down to the boardwalk. It wasn't on her usual route, but she welcomed the cool breeze from the water. Checking her watch she saw she had plenty of time left before she had to be at work, so she walked over to the grassy area and proceeded to do her post-run stretches.

Choosing a bench along the fence separating the boardwalk from the water, she sat down and closed her eyes, taking in the slightly salty air and the breeze that blew strands of loose hair across her face as it cooled her. She was lost in her thoughts and didn't hear the man approach her.

"May I sit next to you?" The polite, husky voice asked, startling her.

"Oh," Sarah exclaimed, her eyes flying open. She blinked a few times to clear away the haze. Standing in front of her was, in her mind, the best looking man she had ever seen. Tall, dark wavy hair, bright welcoming smile, a jawline so sharp it could cut glass. He was wearing a suit, which she thought was a bit odd, seeing as they were practically on the water. Flustered, Sarah cleared her throat, hoping her cheeks weren't on fire. "Um, sure. Go ahead," she told the man, scooting over to give him plenty of room.

"Thank you," he replied, taking a seat. Sarah watched as the stranger sat down next to her. He kept to himself, and seemed intent on staring out at the water and relaxing. Satisfied she wasn't about to be bothered or worse, Sarah looked back to the water as well, attempting to gather her thoughts and compose herself.

"Are you all right?" The man asked, turning to face her. "You seem a bit. . . nervous. I hope it's not because of me," he added, smiling to break the tension.

"Not at all," she replied, having regained herself. "You had just startled me a bit when you arrived, I wasn't paying attention to my surroundings is all, she shrugged. Stupid move, I know. And admitting to a total and complete stranger - even more stupid.

"Well, that's good to hear," he chuckled. Extending his hand he said, "I'm Brian, by the way."

She took his hand. "Sarah."

"Sarah," he mused. "Beautiful name for a beautiful girl. Are you new here? I don't recall seeing you around town much, just on your morning jog." Seeing the expression on her face, he quickly added, "I live along your usual route and have seen you, I'm not a stalker or anything." He held his hands up in defense.

Well, that's a load off my mind, she thought to herself sarcastically. Because everyone who admitted they weren't a stalker, totally wasn't one.

"I, too, enjoy the occasional jog, perhaps we'll run together one morning," he suggested, a hint of hopefulness in his voice.

Not wanting to be rude, Sarah simply nodded her head. "Sure, that sounds like fun." After all, she didn't know this man, other than the fact that his name was Brian and he was incredibly handsome. Besides, she had moved here to get away from men and relationships, not to immediately start up a new one.

They shared the occasional round of small talk, slowly getting to know each other a little. But then they would lapse back into enjoying the silence of the morning. Brian seemed to sense when she needed some time to herself, which she greatly appreciated. She hated having to talk nonstop. Especially when it was about herself. She never knew what to say. How do you know what information to share with strangers? How much was too much? Did they really want to know everything about you? There was really no way to tell.

After a few minutes of grilling each other about their likes and dislikes, the two of them sat in a slightly uncomfortable silence for a while longer, enjoying the comforting sounds and smells coming off the coast.

"Well," Brian said, startling her once again, "this has been a pleasant, exciting morning," he smiled brightly. "Until next time. Have a good day Sarah. It was an absolute pleasure meeting you," he said as he got up and walked away.

"You too," she whispered to his back since he had set off before she could even respond. She felt an odd sort of longing now that he was completely out of view. The air felt cooler in his absence. They had barely spoken to each other, yet Sarah almost missed him. Almost. She shook her head, breathed in the salty air once more, and began the short journey back home to start getting ready for the rest of her day.

Two

"YOU LOOK DIFFERENT," Janet observed as Sarah set her purse down on her desk. Janet worked at the cubicle next to Sarah, and was the closest thing she had to a friend since moving here. The two of them hadn't hung out after work yet, but not for the lack of trying on Janet's part. From the very first day Sarah started working at the small, local newspaper, Janet had been super friendly, gossiping with her, always inviting her out for drinks and such. Sarah had always politely declined though, not feeling ready to mingle yet, for lack of better word. But she did always welcome some girl talk.

"Do I?" Sarah asked, hoping she didn't mean different as in bad.

different as in bad.

Her friend looked her over carefully. "You do,' she

said slowly. Janet snapped her fingers. "I got it. You met a guy, didn't you?"

Oh, Sarah thought to herself. She really hoped no one could see the heat that quickly crept up in her face.

Janet nodded in satisfaction. "You did. I know that look anywhere. You totally met a guy. So . . . spill," she said, tucking her knees up under herself.

This really wasn't a subject that Sarah was comfortable with. "Well," she said rubbing her hand along the back of her neck, "there's not much to tell. Not really. All I really know is that his name is Brian, we talked, but not a lot."

Janet swiveled a bit in her chair. "Okay, so minimal words were exchanged. How did he look, though?"

"Dreamy," Sarah admitted. "He was wearing a suit, very professional looking, had long dark hair-the kind you just want to run your fingers through," she sighed, imagining herself doing just that. She hadn't thought about him this way when they first met, since meeting him unexpectedly had made her a little nervous. But after some time had passed Sarah had found him attractive. Really attractive. She wished she could go back to this morning and get to know him a little better.

"Wow," Janet said, disturbing her mini daydream. "I really wish I would have been with you to see him."

I don't, Sarah thought to herself. Janet was much better looking than she was, and men loved her. If Janet had been with Sarah that morning Brian most likely wouldn't have known she even existed. Janet would have thrown herself right at him, no hesitation. "I ran into him while jogging," Sarah pointed out.

"Ah," Janet replied, her voice edged with disappointment. "I'll probably never get to see him then. You'll never catch me out on a jog. You weird health nuts," she said, shaking her head in amusement.

Sarah couldn't help but laugh. She certainly didn't consider herself a health nut, she enjoyed her fair share of chocolate and cake and other sweet, unhealthy things. And jogging was more of a stress reliever than anything.

"Well," Janet said, "I guess you'll just have to bring him to me then to meet."

"I doubt I'll be seeing him again, but if I do, I suppose we can arrange something," Sarah sighed, rolling her eyes. She made several false promises like this daily. Most of the time she felt bad, like she was being a horrible friend. But then again, she'd feel even worse if she was just saying 'no' all the time.

"And see if he has a friend. A single friend, preferably!"

Sarah shook her head again and smiled.

Three

AFTER WORK SARAH PROMISED, yet again, to sometime soon go out for drinks with Janet. She was thinking maybe this time she'd actually commit. It was about time. She had been pretty much nothing but a hermit since moving here. And although she had gone out of her way to avoid relationships, having a man like Brian, whose looks would make any girl swoon, paying attention to her had given Sarah the boost of confidence she didn't know she had needed. Having Janet being jealous of her for once was just an added bonus.

Heading to the store for some much needed grocery shopping, Sarah found her thoughts drifting back to Brian, with his smile that lit up her morning more than the sun and his dark hair blowing in the breeze.

She sighed again, men weren't the reason she had moved here. Relationship hunting wasn't priority number one. Getting her life back together was.

She browsed the aisles, not sure what she wanted to make for dinner tonight. She wasn't craving anything in particular. There were way too many choices. Spotting a box of her favorite pasta up on the top shelf, she silently cursed herself for being so vertically challenged. All the women in her family were on the short side, and she absolutely hated it. Stretching her arm up while standing on her toes, the box was still just out of reach.

"Need some help?" A familiar husky voice asked from directly behind her.

Sarah turned to face Brian. "Sure," she said with a goofy looking smile on her face. "Two times in one day. This town must be smaller than I thought," she laughed awkwardly. I must sound so stupid, she thought. Stop it, she mentally slapped herself. She was beginning to feel just like a lovestruck teenager. Blushing hard, she mumbled "thanks," as he handed her the box of pasta.

"This is indeed a small town. And you are very

welcome," Brian said. The smile he gave her made her knees weak. Oh, this was one tall, dark, handsome stranger. "Searching for something to make for dinner?" he asked, clearly amused with her embarrassment. "I am as well. I just stopped in after work to find something quick and easy. I'm on my way back to the marina. I have a boat there." Sarah detected a hint of pride in his voice.

"Yeah, I also just got off work and I realized that my fridge and cupboards are practically empty. This trip was long overdue."

"Ah. So, any suggestions for me?" he asked hopefully. "I am the worst in the kitchen. It's a miracle I'm still alive," he joked.

Sarah smiled. "Well, clearly you're doing something right." Her smile faltered and face blazed with embarrassment when she realized that she had said that out loud and not just in her head. "I just mean, um . . ."

"That's all right. I think I know what you meant," he winked. "So, about those suggestions . . ."

Sarah cleared her throat. "Well, it depends on what you like, really. I'm making a simple pasta dish myself."

"That actually sounds perfect," he said.

"Well, would you maybe like to join me tonight?" She found herself asking before she could stop herself. "If you don't have any other plans, I mean."

His eyes lit up. "I was only planning on visiting my boat tonight for some relaxation, but your plan sounds even better." Oh, that smile . . .

"Are you sure? I don't want to take you away from anything."

"Absolutely. Like I said, I was just heading there to relax. I can do that any day."

So the two of them finished grocery shopping together, and Brian helped load the bags into the back of Sarah's car. "Shall I just follow you to your place?" he asked.

Sarah hadn't thought about that. Brian - in her home, and so quickly after they met. He seemed nice though, trustworthy and incredibly comfortable to be around, so she softened a bit. "Sure. Just don't get lost," she joked.

"Oh, I won't. Small town, remember?" he said with a wink as they climbed in their separate cars.

The drive home was more nerve wracking than ever before. Sarah's hands were shaking so badly on the wheel she thought it was a miracle she didn't crash. She nervously pulled into her driveway and waited inside the car until Brian pulled up beside her.

"What a cute little house," Brian commented as he helped unload the car. Sarah shot him a look that said she was slightly offended. He then quickly added, "I didn't mean small as a bad thing, not at all. More. . . cozy. That's the word I was looking for." He had hoped that was enough to redeem himself.

"It is," Sarah offered, "very cozy. It may be a bit on the small side, but it's absolutely perfect since it's just me. I don't need a whole lot of room," she shrugged.

Feeling better, Brian grabbed most of the bags, both to be a gentleman and to allow Sarah to unlock the front door. Most people here, in Bright Wave, left their doors unlocked, for the fear of being robbed was pretty much nonexistent. Everyone here knows and trusts one another. Another reason Sarah was glad for the move. Still, she couldn't bring herself to leave the door unlocked. It would be a hard habit to break.

"You can set the bags down on the table there," Sarah said, referring to the kitchen island. "I'm just going to go wash up real quick and then we can start cooking. Well, I'll start." Her cheeks reddened again.

Brian laughed. "I'll be glad to be of assistance. Just don't expect too much from me, I wouldn't want to burn the house down or anything." He began unpacking the food while Sarah headed down the hall to the bathroom.

She quietly closed and locked the door. Leaning her back against the door, she closed her eyes and wondered what the hell she was doing. She had just met this man, what, hours ago? And here he was, in her house, standing in her kitchen waiting to have dinner with her.

I must be out of my mind, she thought to herself as she walked to the sink to wash her hands. Completely out of my mind.

"Sorry that took so long," Sarah said as she walked back into the kitchen. She saw that the bags were unpacked, folded neatly and placed on the counter. He had left out the ingredients needed for tonight and had them organized on the island, ready to be cooked.

He rubbed the back of his neck. "I, uh, hope you don't mind," he said, gesturing to his handiwork, "I'm kind of big on organizing and thought I'd at least get started. I didn't know where you keep all your utensils and everything or I would have gotten started on the washing and chopping. I didn't feel right just going through your things," he let out a small laugh.

"It's all right. I wouldn't have minded," she laughed. "It's not like there's any secrets in here for you to uncover or anything."

Sarah could feel the tension leaving the room. She was glad for the lighter mood. He laughed as he washed his hands. Sarah handed him the strainer to wash the lettuce for their salads.

They continued the playful banter as they washed

and chopped vegetables, cooked the pasta, and heated up the sauce for their first dinner together.

This was actually her first dinner with anyone since moving here.

Setting the table, Sarah was surprised at how comfortable this all felt already. Having Brian here, setting the table for two instead of the usual one, it all felt . . . right.

Four

"THAT WAS DELICIOUS" Brian said as he wiped the last bit of sauce off his mouth. "Really hit the spot. We make a great team," he laughed.

"That we do," Sarah replied, feeling some of the earlier nervousness creeping back. To distract herself, she got a second bottle of wine out of the fridge. "Refill?"

"Sure, why not?" Brian said. "One more couldn't hurt."

Sarah filled both glasses, and without thinking, suggested they go sit the fireplace in her living room. "It would be more comfortable," she offered, hoping he wasn't thinking she meant anything by that comment. She led him into the living room, but not before Brian quickly rinsed all the dishes and neatly set them in the sink. He really is all about being organized, she thought.

They sat opposite each other and Sarah secretly studied Brian over her wine glass, hoping he wouldn't notice her staring at him. He had strong features, a kind face, he just looked like the kind of person that you could really trust. He was also facing the fire, his eyes sparkling as they caught the light of the dancing flames. She relaxed a bit. This really wasn't so bad after all.

"So how long ago did you move here?" Brian asked, breaking the silence.

"Only a few months ago. I needed a change."

"Ah," he nodded once.

Anticipating his next questions, she said "I moved here from New York. Bright lights, loud noise 24-7, everything was so fast-paced and stressful. It just wasn't . . . me." She shifted in her seat.

"Well, this certainly is a change."

Sarah nodded in agreement. "It is. It's so quiet and peaceful here. I already love it so much." She took a sip of wine, feeling herself loosening up a bit. Closing her eyes, she said, "Moving here was exactly what I needed after . . ." She stopped herself before she revealed too much.

"After what?" Brian asked in a soothing voice.

"Um, just some personal stuff that happened. I don't really want to talk about it right now." Her face was now a deep shade of red, matching the wine.

" Fair enough. So what do you like to do? Besides jogging and picking up strange men for pasta and wine?" he joked.

Sarah laughed so hard wine almost came out of her nose. That would have been embarrassing. "Well," she replied, "I enjoy reading any chance I get. I don't . . . I don't really do much," she admitted with a small chuckle. "I haven't really made any friends yet, I've always been terrible at that. There's one girl at work who I suppose would be the closest thing I actually have to a friend." She broke down laughing again. "Well, now it's me who's rambling."

Brian joined in her laughter. "We're both a couple of nervous wrecks I guess."

"Okay," Sarah said, trying to compose herself. She looked to Brian as she wiped a tear from her eyes. She hadn't laughed like this in years. "You know, I think I'll just go ahead and tell you." She was feeling much more confident now. "Truth is, I had a, I was in a horrible relationship back in New York - controlling, abusive, mostly verbal, the bruises that I did have are pretty much all faded now." The internal scars would remain forever, she thought sadly to herself. "I didn't mean to bring down the mood, because tonight has been amazing. I just get nervous around new people, especially men," she gestured towards Brian. "Not that I think you'll harm me, it's just sort of an automatic response. And I apologize. I finally escaped my ex and immediately moved here. I have no friends or family here, no connections, but at least he can't find me." She stared down at her now empty wine glass, almost ashamed at having unloaded all this on Brian on the first-what was this, date? She wasn't too sure.

Sarah didn't take her eyes off her glass, but she heard Brian stand up and walk over to her. He took the glass out of her hands and set both down on the coffee table. Her breath hitched a little as he took her hands in his own. Kneeling down in front of her, Brian gently tilted her head up so he was able to look into her eyes.

"I am so sorry for what you went through. You don't need to tell me any details, you won't have to relive it."

I do every night in my dreams, Sarah thought to herself.

"No one should ever have to live through that. But I am glad that you found the strength to leave, not many can. You're stronger than you think, Sarah. Don't let what happened hold you back. You're meant for amazing things, I can feel it. And thank you , for trusting me enough to tell me this."

All she felt she could do at this moment was offer him a pathetic smile, Sarah knew that if tried to speak it would end up with her a blubbering, crying mess.

"Would you like me to leave?" Brian asked, misreading her silence.

Clearing her throat, she answered, "No, you can stay. This was just a very hard thing for me to talk about. I've never told anyone else. But thank you, for what you said. It really meant a lot."

Brian stood up and before she could stop herself, Sarah jumped up out of her seat and kissed him. "I'm sorry," she said as she abruptly pulled back.

Brian stepped closer to her, shaking his head. "Don't be. I liked it." He smiled that sexy smile of his, put his hands on either side of her head, and kissed her this time.

Five

"WAIT, WHAT?!" Janet practically yelled. Sarah had just finished telling her everything that had happened last night. She was so excited she couldn't hold it in and just had to tell someone. Janet had barely walked through the door at work when she was told the news. "How and why was I not texted with details the second any of this went down?"

"I'm sorry," Sarah said, realizing she hadn't even thought about it. "Everything just kind of happened so fast and it was one of those living-in-the-moment kinda things, I guess."

"Well, the moment's over, girly. Give me details. I want to know everything." Janet made herself comfortable, expecting a long, detailed story.

"There's not many exciting details . . . we shopped, made and ate dinner together, talked, then kissed."

"Sounds super romantic," Janet said flatly as she rolled her eyes.

Sarah laughed. "We talked, like, really talked. About some pretty deep stuff." Janet opened her mouth to say something but Sarah waved off whatever she was about to say.

"The kiss though . . . how was it?" Janet wriggled her eyebrows.

"It was amazing." Sarah replied with a dreamy look in her eyes as she plopped down in her desk chair.

"It was one of those heart-stopping, breathtaking, world-stops-moving kind of kisses."

"Wow. I have never been more jealous of you, or anything before," Janet said, throwing a scrunched up piece of paper at her. "So not fair though. You do nothing but stay home practically every day and you get the guy. I go out all the time-nothing." She pouted.

Sarah just winked at her friend, which caused a paper fight between the two of them.

"So does this mean you're finally, finally willing to be a socializing individual and come out with me?"

It was Sarah's turn to roll her eyes. "All right, I suppose," she laughed. "Why not tonight after work?

Janet dropped the paper that was in her hand.

"Really? Like, you won't cancel on me for the millionth time?"

"Nope. I am all yours tonight."

"Woo hoo!" Janet yelled, throwing a ball of paper into the garbage can like a basketball. It went straight in. "Score."

Later that day as they were walking out of work, Sarah's phone chimed with an incoming text message. Her face lit up when Brian's face appeared on the screen.

"Let me guess-lover boy?" Janet teased. "I know that goofy look."

"Ha. Ha. But yes," she admitted.

"You should totally invite him out tonight. I need to meet him."

Sarah arched her eyebrows. "Need to?'

"Uh, duh. To make sure he's good enough for you."

"Thought you just wanted us to go out?"

"I do, but he can come too. Kind of a guarantee that you'll actually make it out of the house."

"You have so much faith in me." Sarah shook her head. But opening up to Brian last night had really helped her. She woke up feeling lighter, happier. Less afraid. Almost, but not quite, ready to take on the world. She texted Brian their plan for the night and smiled wide when he accepted.

"He's coming."

"Sweet," Janet replied. Before she got into her car she turned back to Sarah. "Don't forget to dress extra sexy tonight," she winked.

THE DANCE CLUB that Janet had picked happened to be right on the water. It had an outdoor patio where the two women waited for Brian to show up. They sat sipping their drinks and enjoying the breeze. It reminded Sarah of the first time she had met Brian, which suddenly felt like a lifetime ago.

"Hey ladies, care to dance?" Janet and Sarah turned to see two strange men standing in front of them.

"No, thank you," Sarah told them with a sweet smile.

"All right, but if the two of you change your mind we'll be in there, tearing up the dancefloor," one of them said, shaking his hips.

Sarah just nodded to keep herself from laughing in their face, she thought they were a little too cocky.

"You sure you don't want to go with them?" Janet laughed. "They look like fun."

"Very sure."

"Evening ladies," that very familiar, husky voice said. "Beautiful night, isn't it?"

"Hi." Sarah stood up awkwardly and gave him a hug. Turning towards her friend, she introduced the two. "Brian, this is Janet, a friend from work. Janet, this is Brian."

Janet walked over and shook Brian's hand. "Her only friend," she corrected, making Sarah laugh once more.

"Okay, it's true. She's my only friend."

"Well, you must be special then," Brian told her. "She doesn't let many people in from what I can tell." True again.

Janet placed her hands on her hips. "She sure doesn't. Well, it is an absolute pleasure to finally meet you, Brian. Sarah here won't stop gushing about you at work. It's non-stop Brian talk from the time we punch in until the time we punch out."

Brian threw his head back in a deep, sexy laugh. Everything about him seemed to be sexy. "I'm sure she does."

The three of them started the evening off with a couple drinks, then headed for the dancefloor for a bit. While Sarah and Brian danced together, the two men from before caught up with Janet again. They turned out to be pretty harmless, and they all had a great time dancing the night away.

"I need a break." Sarah announced after what seemed like hours of nonstop dancing. As the night went on the club became packed, which made Sarah a little uncomfortable and also sweaty from all of the body heat. She motioned to Janet that she and Brian were headed out for some air. She nodded to her friends and went back to dancing.

Brian lightly placed his hands on Sarah's back and led her outside. "Better?" He asked once they were alone.

She closed her eyes and took in the cool, salty air. "Much. I don't do much clubbing. That was almost overwhelming," she admitted with a nervous laugh.

"That's all right, I don't either. Like you, I mostly keep to myself. I actually spend most of my free time out on the water. I own a small boat down at the marina. It was actually not far from where we first met, which is why I was down there that day in the first place. I sail as often as I can. I guess you could say it's my escape from the world," he sighed.

"Sounds wonderful," Sarah replied. "I absolutely love being by the water. It's hard to explain, but I always feel so at peace and like nothing can go wrong when I'm near the water. It's kind of like my happy place I guess," she laughed.

"Well, if you would like, you should come out with me next weekend. It's when I'm going out sailing next. We can even have a picnic on the water."

Sarah beamed. "I would love that."

"So it's a date," Brian said, and closed in for a kiss.

"Woah, woah. Get a room guys." Neither of them had seen or heard Janet approach them.

"Where are your boyfriends?" Sarah teased, noticing her friend was alone.

"Moved on to someone else when I turned down their offer to go home with both of them. At the same time."

"Gross."

"Tell me about it. So . . . I just know you have been wondering, and Brian, you have my 100% approval to date my friend here," she nodded towards Sarah.

We both laughed. "I got the friend's approval? Yes!" Brian said with both arms in the air triumphantly.

Sarah shook her head. I chose the weirdest people to hang out with.

Seven

WAITING for the weekend to get here was absolute torture. The days crawled by at a snail's pace. Actually, a snail probably moved faster. Sarah and Brian still got together almost daily, they even took up jogging together every morning, but she was really excited to go sailing. This would be the first time ever that she had ever been sailing. Being alone with Brian, out on the water just seemed, to her, like the absolute perfect day.

She had actually really enjoyed her night out with Janet as well, and the two of them would go shopping or out to eat or just go over to one or the other's house to hang out after work all the time. Back in New York Sarah's ex wouldn't allow her to have any friends, so she was learning to love the freedom and companionship that came with having friends.

Moving to Maine turned out to be the best thing Sarah had ever done, even if the circumstances had sucked to begin with. She was learning a great deal about who she was, the true meaning of friendship, and she was falling in love. Falling for a man who was sweet, sexy, cared so much for her as well as her friends. She couldn't believe how much she had been missing out on. In just a short time she had experienced so many new things, and she wouldn't have it any other way.

Now, if only the weekend would hurry up and get here already.